MIDNIGHT
VISITORS

....

A STEAMPUNK SHORT STORY

KEVIN O. MCLAUGHLIN

Role of the Hero Publishing
BOSTON, MA

Role of the Hero Publishing
58 Leo Birmingham Parkway #2
Brighton, MA
www.roleofthehero.com

Publisher's Note: This is a work of fiction. Names, characters, places, and incidents are a product of the author's imagination. Locales and public names are sometimes used for atmospheric purposes. Any resemblance to actual people, living or dead, or to businesses, companies, events, institutions, or locales is completely coincidental.

Ordering Information:
Quantity sales. Special discounts are available on quantity purchases by corporations, associations, and others. For details, contact the "Special Sales Department" at the address above.

Midnight Visitors/ Kevin O. McLaughlin -- 1st ed.
ISBN 978-0692243138

For my grandfather, Henry Diks, and his cat Noelle.
I love you, Grandpa.

Love remembers; love supports. Love defends. But above all else, love overcomes all obstacles. Love is the greatest force of nature.

–Kevin O. McLaughlin

···

A STEAMPUNK SHORT STORY

Noelle opened one eye lazily, viewing the world through the narrowest slit, and let her tail drift down from her nose. She was as tired as a cat could be. It had been a long night, and she knew tonight would be more of the same. She'd more than earned her nap, but Noelle had heard her name called, which would never cease to pique her curiosity, if not her interest.

"Noelle, there you are!" Her person ambled amiably over to where she rested on the windowsill, carefully setting aside the candle he carried to avoid singing her fur. His name was Henry, and he was old but rather wise as these two legged beings went. Not a cat, no. But a good being. He'd taken her in on a cold night in the middle of winter, and given her a spot by his warm fireplace and a name that had something to do with a human celebration. When one of his friends said he should dump her back out in the snow – talking about black cats being bad luck – Henry had scoffed at the notion.

She'd gone on to train him well, these past three years. And somewhere along the line, to the wonder of the foot-free cat she'd been before, she'd become his as much as he was hers.

To illustrate the point, she sat up, looked up at him with blinking eyes, and gave a soft "Mreow?"

"Treats?" Henry asked her.

"Mreow," she replied.

He reached into a pocket of his waistcoat, fishing about for some of the small morsels he regularly carried there for her. He was a good person, and this was a good place. She was glad she'd found it, even if there were...difficulties.

Henry plunked the first tidbit down in front of her nose. She gave it a few dainty sniffs before wolfing it down. Just for appearances, of course. One could never seem to be too eager. It had been work training her human, and she knew better than to let that slip, even for a moment. No matter how fond she had grown.

"You're a good cat," Henry said, laying another treat down for her. She gulped that one down too. "I just don't understand why you won't chase the mice like other cats do!"

He sighed, stroking her fur absently. She purred in response. The answer to his question would have been obvious, if he'd been a cat. But he wasn't, so she had to make due as best she could.

"They were into the grain again last night. I found one bag chewed open, spilled all over the floor of the closet."

Noelle kept up her purring, and he continued stroking her.

"A good cat," Henry said again. He closed his eyes, relaxing. "If you would only deal with the mice, please. I have enough to worry about. My invention must be complete by the end of the week, or the King will withdraw my funding." He opened his eyes again, and Noelle matched his bright blue gaze with her own yellow eyes. "He told me so himself, you know. Me! In an audience with royalty!"

The old man jumped back to his feet, alive with an energy that belied his years. "It's back to work for me, then!" he cried. Noelle canted her head sideways a bit, letting his renewed enthusiasm wash over her like the heat of a sunbeam. "Much to do!" Henry rushed from the room.

Then returned, peeking around the corner of the doorway to smile at Noelle. "And you rest. I am sure you will find a way to solve the problem of our midnight visitors."

With that, he was gone – returned to his workshop upstairs.

Noelle exhaled slowly, settling back into the windowsill. If only he knew how big a problem they really had with midnight visitors. He wouldn't be so worried about the mice, then.

She closed her eyes again. Time to rest. Night would come soon, and she had to be prepared.

Darkness had fallen over the shop. The candles were all extinguished. Henry had been in bed for hours, and asleep for at least a while. Now Noelle stalked through his attic workshop, almost invisible in the pools of shadow.

She froze, listening.

The tiniest sound, a scuffing on the floor mixed with the almost silent whirring of gears. No human could have heard those sounds, but her feline ears could. She held herself completely still.

A flicker of movement.

She pounced, her entire body moving forward in a single bound. She landed atop the small, running thing, catching it betwixt her paws. Her head twisted sideways, jaw opening between her paws and then clamping down hard on the thing.

This was where she had run into trouble, the first couple of times she'd killed these intruders. They looked like mice, but they did not smell or taste like mice, and they were made of metal. Her teeth found poor purchase on the smooth surface, and she couldn't crack the shell. But she had worked out a system.

She flipped the thing over with her teeth, and then worried at each of the frantic little legs, breaking it free from the machine. That done, it wasn't going anywhere, and she looked it over carefully. It was the same as the one she had destroyed last night, and the night before, and the night before that. They'd been stalking Henry's workshop every time darkness fell for almost a fortnight.

They looked like mice, but gleamed if the light hit them. They were the color of Henry's brass candlesticks, smooth on their back, with a little waving wire tail and metal bits for legs. Where the face should have been sat a single glass eye.

Noelle had no idea what they were or where they came from. But they were not Henry's, and she had a strong hunch they were up to no good. Cats always listened to their intuitions.

It was still whirring away inside. She gently bit down on the thing, taking care not to break her teeth on it. The underbelly was less resistant, and her jaws pushed it inward. She felt something break inside it, and the whirring stopped. It was dead.

She picked it up in her mouth and carried it to a corner of the workshop, where there was a small hole in one of the wall boards. The hole went right into the space between the walls, and was just big enough for the little devices after she'd broken them. With a few shoves from her nose, the thing joined the other dozen or so she'd deposited in the same manner. She heard a soft clink as it hit another of the broken not-mice.

More scuttling. This time from Henry's workbench, where he worked on the thing he called his 'masterpiece' every day. Frankly, all Noelle saw was a big box. But it was important to Henry, so it was important to her as well. She padded quickly across the room toward the sounds. There had never been more than one not-mouse in a night, before. Now she could hear two more of them.

She reached the first. It was trying to scurry up the wooden leg of the work table, metal legs biting into the wood with each step, slowly making its way upward. That one glass eye was locked facing upward, and Noelle didn't think they had any other senses. It never had a chance – she dashed forward, and batted it hard with one paw.

The not-mouse flew from the table leg and smacked hard against the wall. The whirring stopped. The things were fragile as a cobweb.

The third not-mouse had used the extra few moments to climb out of her easy reach, though, and was about to get to the top of the work bench. Noelle didn't know what they could do, if they actually reached Henry's invention. She didn't need to know. It was enough that they were up to something that would harm Henry.

She leapt to the top of the table, arriving in front of the not-mouse just as it clambered over the edge. It saw her and dashed sideways, trying to scurry past her. She pounced, but this one was smart, and dodged out of the way of her paws just in time.

It tore past her, racing across the bench toward Henry's invention. Noelle turned on a dime and was after it. It couldn't see her from behind, and a second pounce caught it. With her teeth, she repeated the process she'd used to disable the first one. But her mind was elsewhere.

Three in one night? There had never been three of the not-mice before. Something had changed. Her jaws clamped closed on the little metal shell, stopping the whirring gears inside, while her senses reached out, straining to be alert to the smallest sound.

The tinkling of glass, from downstairs.

Distraction. The extra mice were there to keep her busy, keep her occupied, keep her away from Henry. She dropped the broken not-mouse, and sprang from the table, feet already moving as she hit the ground running. She raced down the stairs and into a scene out of nightmare.

Henry had real glass windows in his house. She adored them, because they kept the heat in but let her see outside. But now she wished he had used something less fragile. The window in the front door was shattered, and something was clambering through.

It dropped to the ground and scuttled toward her on six legs. In front of it waved two huge claws almost as big as her head, snapping open and closed with the sharp hiss of air and the scent of burnt oil. Behind the terror lashed a tail twice as long as her own, with a wicked barb on the end. She'd never seen anything like it, and something deep inside her heart quailed at the sight of the thing. She backed up a step, sinking into the shadows.

It snapped its claws at her once more, than turned toward Henry's room. It was satisfied, perhaps, that it had cowed her. It stalked forward, placing each foot carefully, quietly stalking toward its sleeping prey.

With growing horror, Noelle realized that she could hear a whirring noise from the thing. The same whirring that the not-mice made. This was another not-thing – a construct. Noelle had seen some toys like the not-mice before. Little windup things, clockwork devices that walked for a bit before running down. Henry's friend had shown them off – the same man who'd suggested that Henry rid himself of her.

Noelle sniffed the air, and yes, there it was. She'd never scented him on the smaller not-mice, but this thing was bigger, and his scent was clear as day on the thing. She knew who had made it, who had sent it.

Henry's not-friend had sent it to kill him.

Noelle growled a warning, stepping out of the darkness again. Her ears were flat against her skull. Her hair puffed out around her. The thing stopped in its tracks. It whirled, turning toward her. Unlike the not-mice, this thing had many eyes. It could see all around itself. She glared into one of the glass eyes, imagining that she could see Henry's not-friend staring back at her through it. Perhaps he could see her; she didn't know, and it didn't matter for now.

She jumped toward the thing, hissing. It snapped claws in her face, pulling her up short. She dodged sideways, guided by instinct, and the tail stinger slammed into the floor where she'd been a moment before.

The construct took a moment to recover from the tail strike, and she used that time to reach in with claws out, striking at the eyes. Her paw met unyielding metal, her claws not even leaving scratches on the smooth surface. Noelle leaped back, dodging those deadly claws again.

She dove in, biting at one of the legs, but it was too well attached. The thing wheeled in place, dragging her with it as she clung to the metal leg. She saw the futility, and rolled clear just before the stinger struck the floorboards again.

It was strong, well armored, but it was much slower than her. She needed to find a way to use that to her advantage. Even as she had the thought, an idea came to her.

She turned tail and ran for the kitchen, making sure she stayed slow enough that she made a tempting target. The thing dashed after her, legs pumping furiously to drive it down the hall. She fled across the tiled kitchen floor, making a beeline for the closet that Henry had left open for her, so that she could get in to hunt mice. If only the mice were as reliable tonight as the clockwork not-mice, perhaps she had a chance.

But she'd misjudged the construct's speed. It caught up with her as she was coming around the closet door, claw reaching out toward her. Noelle poured on the speed, trying to get clear of that deadly claw – but it snagged her tail. She yowled, stopped short.

The claw had a grip on her tail, and the thing dragged her back along the floor a few inches. She tried to grip with her claws, but there was no purchase on the tile. Noelle looked back over her shoulder, saw the stinger descending, and the world seemed to slow for a moment. She saw the bright metal blade of the stinger grow ever larger. Noelle had to move, or die.

She rolled, hard, yowling with the pain as her tail twisted in the claw. Suddenly, she was free! Her tail felt like it was on fire, and she lashed it experimentally, only to realize that it was gone. The claw had cut through her tail entirely. All that remained was a few inches of stub.

Ignoring the wound for the moment, she hissed a challenge at the thing and ran into the closet.

It followed.

Inside, Noelle leaped to the top of Henry's piled bags of dried foodstuff. She turned then, to watch the thing's progress. It didn't fare as well.

The real mice had been busy again tonight, and Noelle had never been so grateful to the tasty creatures. They'd torn open a bag of rice near the bottom of the pile, scattering the contents across the closet floor. The construct entered the small space moving at high speed, hit the rice, and lost its footing. It crashed to the floor, legs working in an attempt to get back up, and then losing their purchase again.

That wouldn't last long, but for the moment, it was precisely where Noelle wanted it to be.

She slipped behind a heavy bag near the top of the pile, sliding between it and the wall, and pushed.

The bag tipped. She pushed harder, and it tumbled down, end over end, to smack onto the top of the flailing construct below. There was a crunch as twenty pounds of flour impacted delicate clockwork components, but the thing was better built than the not-mice. It kept moving, albeit slower and with less surety.

Noelle was fine with that. She growled in her throat as she slowly stalked her way down from her perch. This thing had cost her a tail. She'd finish it...slowly.

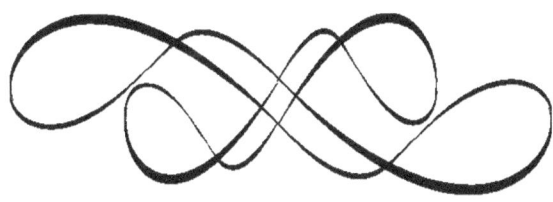

Some time later, Noelle finally settled into bed at Henry's feet. It felt good to rest, but she thought she ought to stick near him, in case his not-friend sent anything else. She curled into a ball, washing the clipped stub where her tail used to be, mourning the loss of its graceful length. With a start, she realized that although she missed the tail, she'd lose it again for this person.

The thought filled her with satisfaction, and she rumbled deep in her throat.

Tomorrow would likely be another interesting day. She thought Henry expected to find a dead mouse somewhere, evidence of her kill. She hadn't had the heart or energy to hunt any of the real mice after the night she'd had. But instead, she'd hauled the clawed construct from the closet after she'd ensured it was thoroughly disabled. It had been heavier than she'd thought, but she'd laid it at the foot of Henry's bed anyway.
The look on his face in the morning would be worth it.

The End.

ABOUT THE AUTHOR

When not practicing hobbies which include sailing, constructing medieval armor, and swinging swords at his friends, Kevin McLaughlin can usually be found in his home near Boston. Kevin's award-winning short fiction is now available in digital form at all major ebook retailers. His urban fantasies "By Darkness Revealed" and "Ashes Ascendant" are available in ebook and print. His latest effort, the STARSHIP series, is ongoing.